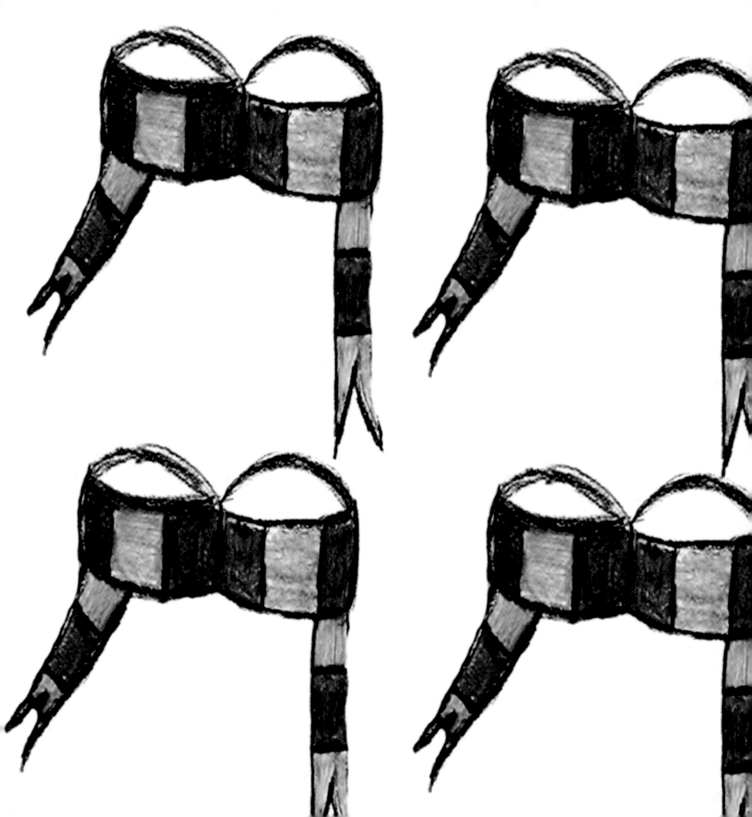

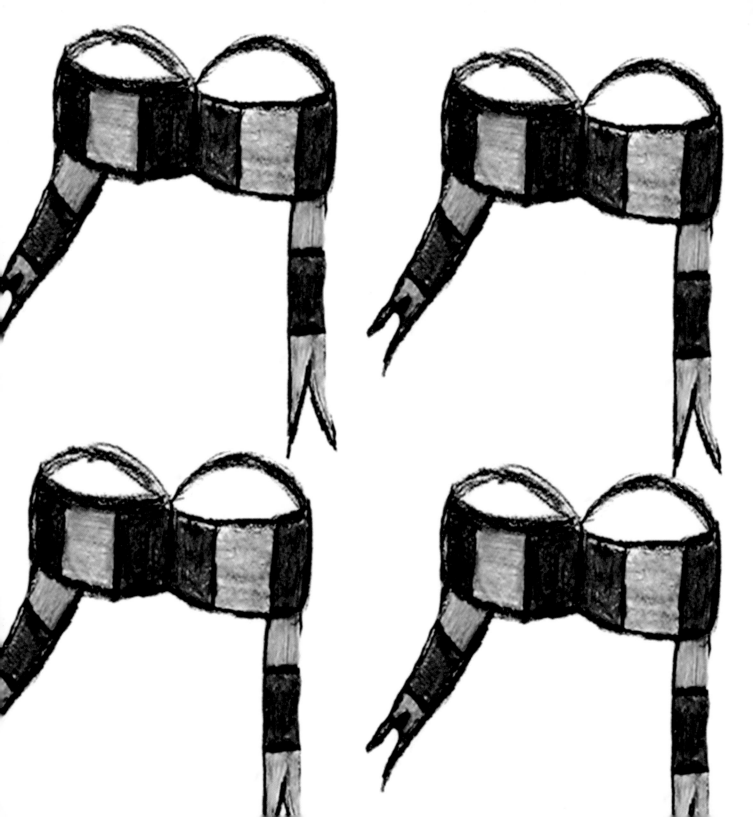

This book is dedicated to my beloved sister and best friend. For all the years of unconditional love and support.

My side of the scarf

Carmen Parets Luque

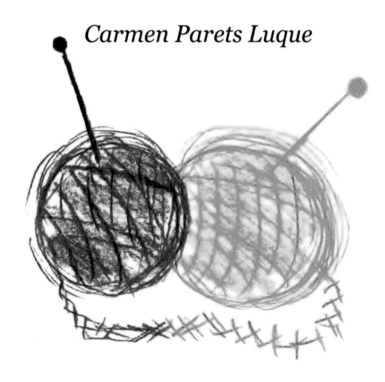

This story doesn't begin like other stories, with *"Once upon a time..."* but with a very important question.

A question that is said with love, like this, whispering in the ear very softly:

"Do you want to be my friend?"

And when Oliver and Violet met, they became best friends in the world.

So much so that they became inseparable. They went everywhere together and got along well.

When adults get married, they say they've found their better half, but when two true friends meet, they've finally found their half scarf.

Oliver and Violet's scarf was small at the beginning, it was made of few loose threads... but it grew as time passed and their friendship grew more and more.

Everything was going well so long as they wanted to play the same game, but when they wanted different things, they began to have problems and the scarf seemed to break.

When they fought, they each wanted to be right and didn't listen to each other. They formed a tremendous tangle which made it difficult to see and they couldn't undo it.

What a mess! Each wanted to choose the game.
What could they do now?

Well, the only way is to calm down, listen to each other and use the magic words: "Please, Sorry and Thank You."

Whenever one of them was sad, the other would lend a little bit of scarf, giving all their love, kisses and hugs.

Between laughs and games, their scarf grew.

Although they liked different things, they respected each other and remained friends as always.

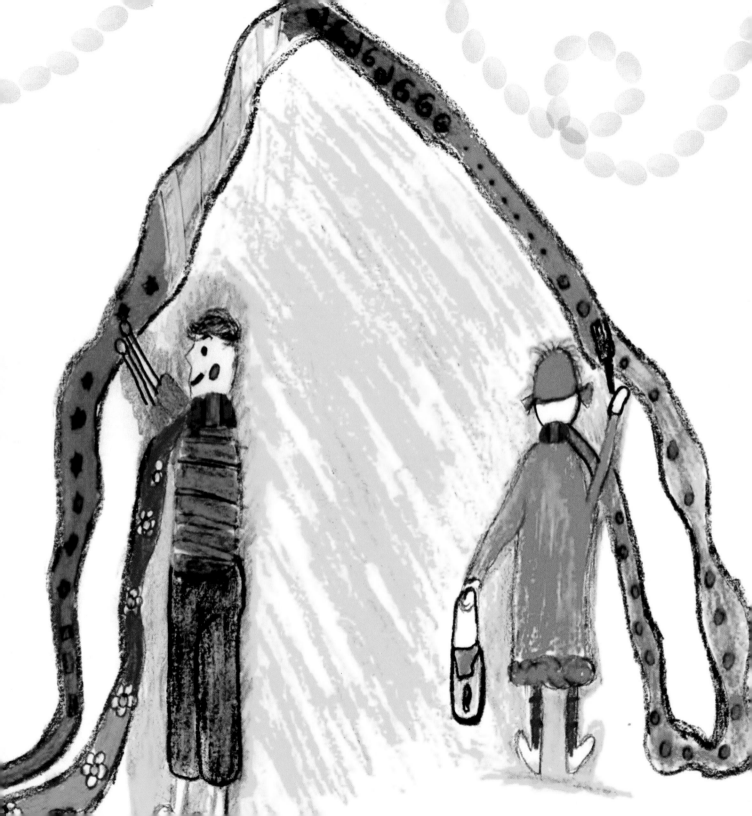

Though the many other friendships they would have.
They never stopped being friends because the scarf always
had room for one more.

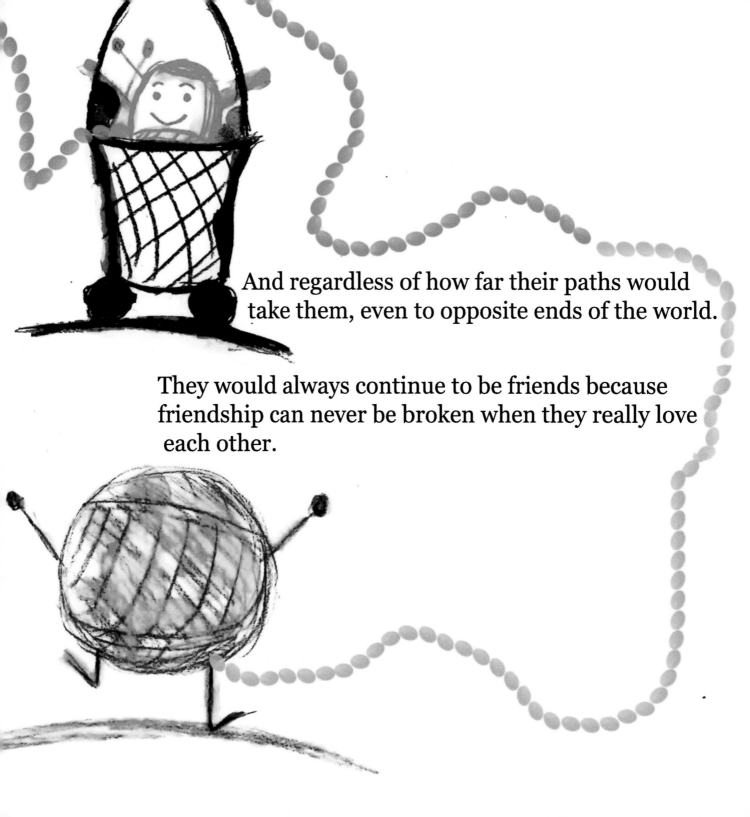

And regardless of how far their paths would take them, even to opposite ends of the world.

They would always continue to be friends because friendship can never be broken when they really love each other.

Other Children's Books.

1. Naia The Witch .

Children's picture book for back to school and first day of preschool for children between 3-6.
Naia is a naughty witch who doesn't want to go to school like other good witches.
You know that will happen?.
You'll find out when you read this story.

2. Paula and her Multi-coloured hair.

A book about feelings for children between 3-6: Pre- to Beginning Readers.
'Paula and her Multi-coloured Hair' is a children's picture book about the most basic human feelings:
joy, sadness, anger and fear.
Through the changes in Paula's hair, we are visually giving a name to the emotions we feel.
Beginning with asking ourselves questions such as... 'What does it cause us that emotion?',
'What does it make us feel?', and 'What should we do?'
we provide answers or solutions for each type of emotion.
In this way, children can learn to identify and manage their emotions in a healthy way.

3. A handful of buttons.

Not all families are the same. Each family is different, unique and special.
This is the beginning of a children's book about family diversity.
What types of families are there? and What special thing makes them a family?
These are some of the answers we want to offer to encourage tolerance towards others.

Made in the USA
Middletown, DE
03 November 2019